How do I use this scheme?

Key Words with Peter and Jane has three parallel series, each containing twelve books. All three series are written using the same carefully controlled vocabulary. Readers will get the most out of **Key Words** with Peter and Jane when they follow the books in the pattern 1a, 1b, 1c; 2a, 2b, 2c and so on.

• Series a
gradually introduces and repeats new words.

• Series b
provides further practice of these same words, but in a different context and with different illustrations.

• Series c
uses familiar words to teach **phonics** in a methodical way, enabling children to read increasingly difficult words. It also provides a link to writing.

LADYBIRD BOOKS

UK | USA | Canada | Ireland | Australia
India | New Zealand | South Africa

Ladybird Books is part of the Penguin Random House group of companies
whose addresses can be found at global.penguinrandomhouse.com.

www.penguin.co.uk   www.puffin.co.uk   www.ladybird.co.uk

First published 1964
This edition 2009, 2014, 2016
Copyright © Ladybird Books Ltd, 1964
001

A CIP catalogue record for this book is
available from the British Library

ISBN: 978-1-409-30124-0

Printed in China

Key Words

with Peter and Jane

6b   We like to help

written by W. Murray
illustrated by M. Aitchison

Here are our friends Peter and Jane, with their Mum and Dad.

Our friends are off to the sea in their car. They will be there soon. They can see the sea now as they look down.

"There it is," says Jane, as she looks out of the car. "There is the sea, and there are the boats on it."

new words
friends   their   day

4

"I want to be down there," says Peter.
"I like to be in a boat on the sea."

The brother and sister talk about the
things they are going to do.

"I want to see all our friends," says
Jane.

"I want to be out in the sun all day,"
says her brother. "I want to go into the
sea and to go out in a boat."

The next day the children go down to see their friend Tom. They like him and he likes them. Tom is at work on his big boat, down by the sea. He has two boats, a big one and a little one.

"It's good to see you," he says to Peter and Jane. "I have to work on my big boat. Do you want to help me?"

"Yes," says Peter, "we want to help you, and then we want to go on the water."

They talk to Tom as they help him with his work on his boat. They tell him about the things they want to do, and he tells them about the sea.

Tom likes to talk to them about the sea and about his boats.

7

Peter looks into the big boat. "Look at this," he says to Jane. "Tom can eat in here, or go to bed if he wants to."

Jane looks into the boat. "Yes," she says, "it's like a little house. It must be fun to live in there."

Tom tells them he lives in his big boat some of the time. He says that when it is hot he likes to live by the sea.

"You can go into the boat if you like," he says to the two children. "You can see where I eat and go to bed."

"Thank you," says Peter. Then he says to Jane, "Come on, let's get into the boat. It will be fun to see where Tom lives."

"Yes," says Jane, "I'll come."

new words

if   live   time   when   hot

Peter gets up on the boat and then he helps Jane to get up.

"It's a big boat," Peter says. "I like it very much."

"Yes," says Jane, "I like it up here."

"I want to have a boat like this, one day," says Peter.

"You can have a big boat like this when you're a man," says Jane.

She puts a hat on Peter. It is Tom's hat.

"There you are," she says. "You look like a man now."

The children play on Tom's boat. Then Jane says, "I'll do some more work for Tom. Help me, Peter."

Peter helps Jane. "Tom is good to us," he says, "so we'll help him."

Tom looks up at the two children. "Thank you very much," he says.

new words
very   much   hat

The children have a good time on Tom's boat. Tom has said they can have a look round.

"Let's go down now," says Jane. "I want to see where Tom eats." The brother and the sister go down.

"Have you been down here before?" Peter asks Jane.

"No, I haven't been here before," Jane says. She looks round and says, "Here's a fish, and I can see that Tom has apples and cake and milk."

Peter looks out at Tom. "We must not let him do all the work. We must go and help him," he says.

"Yes," Jane says, "but I want to come again. I like it down here very much. Let's go up now. It's very hot down here."

new words
round   been   before

13

The next day the children are out in the sun again. They are by the sea with their friends.

They all like to play games. They run and jump, and play with a big ball. It is hot, but they like it to be hot.

When it gets very hot they go into the water. They all like to get wet in the sea.

"It's fun to get wet when you are hot," says Peter.

"Yes, I like it very much," says Jane.

After they have been in the water they run round again, and then Jane wants to sit down.

"I don't want to sit down," says Peter. "I want to make things. You sit down and see what I can make."

new words
wet   don't

Today Peter and Jane go to see Tom. He is by his big boat.

"Do you want us to help you with your work again?" asks Peter.

"No, there's no more work to do on the boat," says Tom.

All three of them look at the boat.

"I like the look of it now," says Peter.

"Yes, so do I," says Jane.

"Do you want to go on the water today?" asks Tom.

"Yes, please," say Peter and Jane.

Then Tom tells them that they must help him to put the boat on the water.

All three of them put the boat on the water. Then Tom gets on the boat and he helps the children on.

"We can go now," he says.

The children have not been on the water before in this big boat.

new words

today   your   three

Tom and the two children are on the boat.

Peter says, "Away we go. We're going out to sea."

Jane looks at the other boats as they go by. She can see other boys and girls on them.

Then Tom lets Jane help him with the boat. He tells her what to do and she does it.

new words
does   birds   fly

"You be the look-out," says Tom to Peter. "Tell us what you see." Peter does as Tom tells him.

Some birds fly by. Peter looks up at the birds as they fly by the boat.

Then Peter says, "Look, I can see a boy in danger. He's in the sea. We must help him."

Tom sees that the boy is in danger. "Good boy, Peter," he says.

All of them can see the boy in the water. He is by his own boat. He is in danger.

Tom knows what to do. He makes his boat go to the boy in the water. Then he pulls the boy from the water. Tom pulls him into his big boat.

Peter wants to help if he can. He gets the boy's hat from the water. He helps Tom with the boy's boat.

The boy is very wet. Jane makes him sit down, and looks after him.

The boy thanks them very much for the help.

"I was going to fish," he says, "but I don't want to now. I want to go home to my mother and father."

"I'll take you home to your mother and father," Tom says.

new words

own mother father

Tom's big boat pulls the little boat after it. The boy who was in the water is in Tom's boat with Peter and Jane.

Jane gives the boy some hot milk. "We'll soon get you to your own home," she says. "Your mother and father will want to know all about this."

When they get out of the boat Peter runs to tell his own father about the boy in the sea. Peter's father comes with his car to take the boy home.

They all go in the car to the boy's house. Here they see the boy's father and mother. Tom tells them that he had to pull their boy out of the water.

The father and mother thank Tom and Peter and Jane very much for their help.

The children have to go home today.
Here they are with Dad and Mum in
their car. As they go by the boats they
can see Tom.

"We'll see you again soon, Tom," they
say.

"I don't want to go home," says Peter
to Jane.

"What about all your friends at home?"
asks Mum.

"Yes, I want to see them all again," says Jane. "I want to see Pam at the farm, and the children next door."

"Yes, I want to see my best friend Bob," says Peter. "I can tell him all about Tom and his boats."

Jane says, "We must tell all our friends about the boy we had to pull out of the water. He was very wet. I had to give him hot milk."

new words
Pam door best Bob

Peter is home again. He has come to see his best friend Bob who lives next door.

He finds Bob at work. He is going to make a doll's house for his little sister Molly.

Bob looks up as Peter comes in.

"Have you had a good time away at the sea?" he asks.

"Yes," says Peter. "We had fun in the sea with a big boat.

"What's this?" he asks.

"This is going to be a doll's house for my little sister Molly," says Bob. "I want to make a big one so that her dolls can go in it. My father will help me. You can help me if you want to."

"Yes, please, Bob. I want to help you very much," says Peter.

---

new words

finds doll's dolls Molly

It is the afternoon of the next day. Here are the two boys at Bob's house. They are at work on the doll's house again. They like to make things.

Mr Green has put in the door and the windows. Now the boys put on the top of the doll's house.

"We'll make it red," says Bob. "Molly likes red."

Then Molly comes in with her baby doll. The little girl sees the doll's house. Bob tells her that it is for her.

"Good," she says. "It's for me. It's my doll's house. I want to put my dolls in it." Molly loves all her dolls.

"She will have fun with it," says Peter.

"Yes," says Bob, "and it'll be fun for us to see her play."

Here is Molly with her doll's house. It is red now. She saw the boys make it for her. She likes it very much. Molly plays with the doll's house every day.

The little girl has four dolls of her own. One is a baby doll. She likes the baby doll best.

She has put every doll into the doll's house so that they look out of the four windows.

Now Molly wants to put the cat in her doll's house. She finds the cat and puts it in with her baby doll. The cat loves to play with Molly.

Molly talks to the dolls and the cat. She asks them if they like their doll's house. Then she says she is going to give them some tea.

new words

every   four

This is the garden of Mr and Mrs Green who live next door to Peter and Jane. It is a big garden. Mr and Mrs Green's two girls play in the garden. The dog Pat is here.

It is very hot this afternoon. Molly is hot and her sister Mary is hot. The dog is hot so he sits by a tree out of the sun. The cat is up the tree.

Mary puts some water on her sister. Molly likes it and asks her to do it again. The two girls have fun with the water.

Peter and Bob are not here. Bob keeps rabbits and the boys are with the rabbits now. Bob looks after the rabbits every day. Peter likes to help him.

new words

garden   Mrs   Mary

The two boys are in the garden now.
They saw Mary and Molly play with the
water.

Peter says to Bob, "Let's play like that.
It's very hot. Let's play with the water."

Bob says, "Yes, we will. I know what
to do."

He gets up the tree. Peter is by the
tree. He looks up.

"Don't look up, Peter," says Bob. "I
want to put some water on you."

Peter looks down, and Bob puts water on him.

"This is fun," says Peter. "I'll do it to you now." Bob gets down, and Peter gets up the tree. Peter puts water on Bob. They like to play with water in the hot sun.

The dog Pat looks on. Then Peter puts some water on him.

This is the farm where Pam lives with her mother and father. Her father keeps cows, pigs and horses. It is a big farm. He lets Pam look after some of the horses. She likes to do this.

There is no school today and Jane has come to the farm to see her friend Pam. Here they are with two horses. The girls love horses.

Pam helps Jane up onto one of the horses and then she gets up onto the other. "Come on," she says. "Let's go."

The horses walk by the trees. "Do you like it, Jane?" asks Pam.

"Yes," says Jane, "and the horses like it as much as we do."

It is a hot day, but it is not hot by the trees.

Here are the girls again, on their horses. They have come away from the trees now.

They stop the two horses to look down the hill.

"I love all this," says Pam. "I love the trees and the flowers. Look at the birds up there."

"Yes," says Jane. Then she says, "I can see men at work on the farm."

"Do you want to take some eggs when you go home?" asks Pam.

"Yes, please," says Jane. "I'll give some of them to my grandmother. I'll be going to see her when I get home."

She tells Pam that she likes to help her grandmother and grandfather because she loves them and because they are old.

The girls and the horses go on.

"I want a horse like this," says Jane.

---

new words

eggs grandmother

grandfather because old

Peter and Jane go to the home of their grandmother and grandfather.

Grandfather is at home in his chair by the fire. He likes to sit in his chair and read for some time every day. Grandmother is in her garden with her flowers. Grandmother and Grandfather do not go out much because they are old. They like it when Peter and Jane come to see them.

new word
gave

Peter and Jane walk down the street to the shops. Jane has a bag and Peter has a ball.

The children get some sweets and some toys. Then they have to get some things for their grandmother. They talk about the things which they have to get.

"Do we want eggs?" asks Peter.

"No," says Jane, "I gave Grandmother some eggs from the farm."

Peter and Jane have been to the shops. They get on a bus to go to their grandmother's and grandfather's house.

They look out of the bus as they go up the street. The children see a train in the station as they go by. Then they go by the Police station, and see a Police car there.

They have tea with their grandfather and grandmother and help with the work in the house.

After this, Grandfather makes some things for Jane's doll's house. He makes a little bed for Jane's doll Ann. "Ann will like this," says Jane. "Thank you very much."

Dad comes in the car to take the children home,

"Look what Grandfather gave me,"
says Jane.

"Grandmother gave me some apples
from the garden," says Peter.

new word
Ann

Jane talks about her school and her teacher.

"I like our teacher," she says. "She is good to all the children. She helps us to read. She gave me this to read at home." Jane reads to Peter.

"Yes," says Peter. "We all like school and we all like our teacher. I like to draw for her. I want to draw now."

"I want to read to Ann," says Jane. She puts her doll Ann on a chair and reads to her.

Peter draws. He draws Jane on a horse, and three or four birds in a tree. Then he draws an old man with a dog.

"I'll take this to school," he says. "I want to let my teacher see this."

new word
teacher

Here is Jane with her best friend Mary. The boys are not here. The two girls are in Mrs Green's garden. Mrs Green is Mary's mother. Jane likes to play with Mary, and Mary likes to play with Jane.

Today they want to play with their dolls. They get some water for their game. Mary puts her doll into the water, and then Jane puts hers in. The two girls have fun as they play with the dolls and the water.

The cat is with them, but she does not like the water. She wants the birds, but she finds that they fly away from her.

Mr and Mrs Green come to see the girls. Then Mr and Mrs Green go out in their car. They are going to the shops.

Peter and Jane go round to the garden next door. Their friends next door are away, and they want Peter and Jane to look after their garden for them.

Jane looks for the cat. She is going to give her some milk. When the cat sees the milk she jumps down from a tree.

Peter says, "The sun is down now, so I'll water the flowers." He puts some water on the garden.

"Don't get wet," says Jane, "and please don't let the water get on the cat. She doesn't like it. She will not have her milk if you do."

"I'll water our own garden after this," says Peter. "Then we must see to the rabbits."

"I like to help our friends like this," says Jane.

The children are home from school and Dad is home from work. They have had tea with Mum.

Dad tells Mum about his day at work. Then he talks to the children.

Peter tells Dad about their work in the garden next door.

"We have to look after the garden because our friends are away," he says.

"We like to do it," says Jane.

"The cat doesn't like it when I water the flowers," says Peter. "If the water gets on her she runs up a tree."

The children know they will soon go to bed.

"I want to read to you before I go to bed," Jane says to Mum. "I like to read to you, and I like to read to my teacher."

New words used in this book

Total number of new words: 53
Average repetition per word: 14